This dragon book belongs to:

....

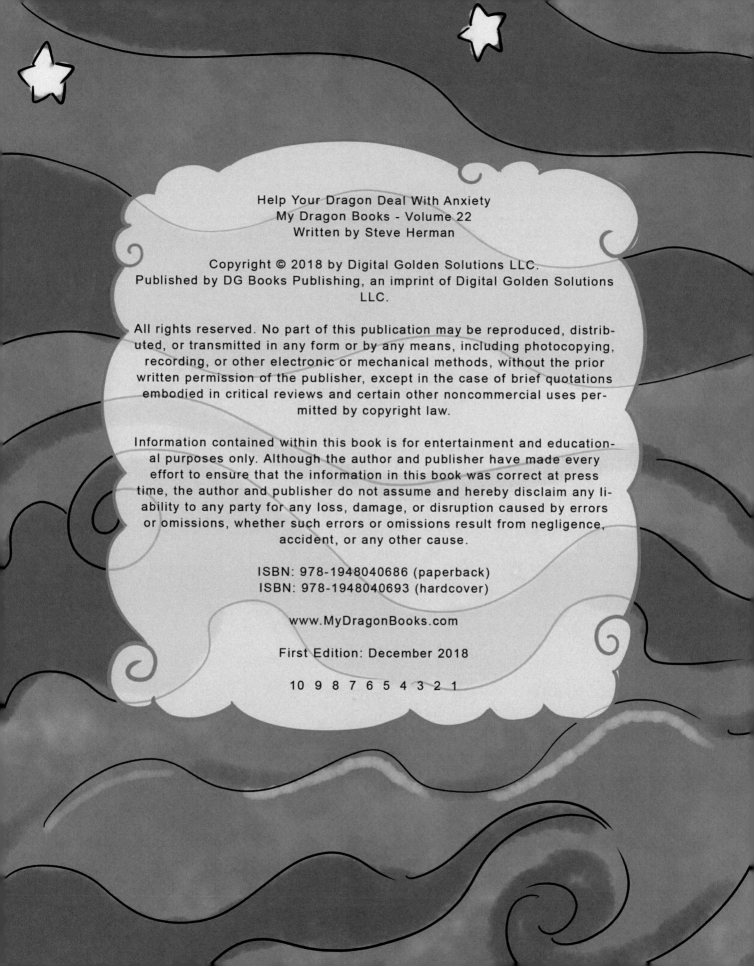

Help Your Dragon Deal With Anxiety
My Dragon Books - Volume 22
Written by Steve Herman

ISBN: 978-1948040686 (paperback)
ISBN: 978-1948040693 (hardcover)

www.MyDragonBooks.com

First Edition: December 2018

10 9 8 7 6 5 4 3 2 1

"I'm scared I may forget," he cried,
"the lessons that I've learned!"
He paced the floor and wrung his hands –
Diggory was concerned.

Diggory Doo plays basketball;
his team is not too bad,
But every night before a game,
Diggory Doo got sad;

"*What if* I shoot and miss?" he cried.
"*What if* we lose the game?
What if my coach gets mad at me
and says that I'm to blame?!"

Diggory Doo loves camping trips; he's handy, I'll admit
To huff and puff a dragon flame to keep the campfire lit.

But when he was a little guy, he'd worry and complain, "Our weekend plans will all be ruined, if it begins to rain!"

Diggory Doo got anxious
when he had to get a shot
Or go to see the doctor.
He would cry, "I'd rather not!"

WHAT IF I CAN !

Now when he's feeling anxious, Diggory Doo has tools to choose - For any stressful situation, he simply just pick one of these techniques to use

Sing along with Diggory Doo and Drew at
www.MyDragonBooks.com/AnxietySong